THE LAST LION AND OTHER TALES

THE LAST LION AND OTHER TALES

VICENTE BLASCO IBÁÑEZ

AN IBÁÑEZ BOOK

AN IBÁÑEZ BOOK

Published by Wildside Press, LLC
www.wildsidebooks.com

CONTENTS

THE LAST LION

SCARCELY had the meeting of the honorable guild of *blanquers* come to order within its chapel near the towers of Serranos, when Señor Vicente asked for the floor. He was the oldest tanner in Valencia. Many masters recalled their apprentice days and declared that he was the same now as then, with his white, brush-like mustache, his face that looked like a sun of wrinkles, his aggressive eyes and cadaverous thinness, as if all the sap of his life had been consumed in the daily motions of his feet and hands about the vats of the tannery.

He was the only representative of the guild's glories, the sole survivor of those *blanquers* who were an honor to Valencian history. The grandchildren of his former companions had become corrupted with the march of time; they were proprietors of large establishments, with thousands of workmen, but they would be lost if they ever had to tan a skin with their soft, business-man's hands. Only he could call himself a *blanquer* of the old school, working every day in his little hut near the guild house; master and toiler at the same time, with no other assistants than his sons and grandchildren; his workshop was of the old kind, amid sweet domestic surroundings, with neither threats of strikes nor quarrels over the day's pay.

The centuries had raised the level of the street, converting Señor Vicente's shop into a gloomy cave.

The door through which his ancestors had entered had grown smaller and smaller from the bottom until it had become little more than a window. Five stairs connected the street with the damp floor of the tannery, and above, near a pointed arch, a relic of medieval Valencia, floated like banners the skins that had been hung up to dry, wafting about the unbearable odor of the leather. The old man by no means envied the *moderns*, in their luxuriously appointed business offices. Surely they blushed with shame on passing through his lane and seeing him, at breakfast hour, taking the sun,—his sleeves and trousers rolled up, showing his thin arms and legs, stained red,—with the pride of a robust old age that permitted him to battle daily with the hides.

Valencia was preparing to celebrate the centenary of one of its famous saints, and the guild of *blanquers*, like the other historic guilds, wished to make its contribution to the festivities. Señor Vicente, with the prestige of his years, imposed his will upon all the masters. The *blanquers* should remain what they were. All the glories of the past, long sequestrated in the chapel, must figure in the procession. And it was high time they were displayed in public! His gaze, wandering about the chapel, seemed to caress the guild's relics; the sixteenth century drums, as large as jars, that preserved within their drumheads the hoarse cries of revolutionary Germania; the great lantern of carved wood, torn from the prow of a galley; the red silk banner of the guild, edged with gold that had become greenish through the ages.

All this must be displayed during the celebration, shaking off the dust of oblivion; even the famous lion of the *blanquers*!

The *moderns* burst into impious laughter. The lion, too?... Yes, the lion, too. To Señor Vicente it seemed a dishonor on the part of the guild to forget that glorious beast. The ancient ballads, the accounts of celebrations that might be read in the city archives, the old folks who had lived in the splendid epoch of the guilds with their fraternal camaraderie,—all spoke of the *blanquers'* lion; but now nobody knew the animal, and this was a shame for the trade, a loss to the city.

Their lion was as great a glory as the silk mart or the well of San Vicente. He knew very well the reason for this opposition on the part of the *moderns*. They feared to assume the rôle of the lion. Never fear, my young fellows! He, with his burden of years, numbered more than seventy, would claim his honor. It belonged to him in all justice; his father, his grandfather, his countless ancestors, had all been lions, and he felt equal to coming to blows with anybody who would dare dispute his right to the rôle of the lion, traditional in his family.

With what enthusiasm Señor Vicente related the history of the lion and the heroic *blanquers*. One day the Barbary pirates from Bujia had landed at Torreblanca, just beyond Castellón, and sacked the church, carrying off the Shrine. This happened a little before the time of Saint Vicente Ferrer, for the old tanner had no other way of explaining history than by dividing it into two periods; before and after the Saint.... The population, which was scarcely moved by the raids of the pirates, hearing of the abduction of pale maidens with large black eyes and plump figures, destined for the harem, as if this were an inevitable misfortune, broke into cries of grief upon learning of the sacrilege at Torreblanca.

The churches of the town were draped in black; people went through the streets wailing loudly, striking themselves as a punishment. What could those dogs do with the blessed Host? What would become of the poor, defenseless Shrine?... Then it was that the valiant *blanquers* came upon the scene. Was not the Shrine at Bujia? Then on to Bujia in quest of it! They reasoned like heroes accustomed to beating hides all day long, and they saw nothing formidable about beating the enemies of God. At their own expense they fitted out a galley and the whole guild went aboard, carrying along their beautiful banner; the other guilds, and indeed the entire town, followed this example and chartered other vessels.

The Justice himself cast aside his scarlet gown and covered himself with mail from head to foot; the worthy councilmen abandoned the benches of the Golden Chamber, shielding their paunches with scales that shone like those of the fishes in the gulf; the hundred archers of la Pluma, who guarded *la Señera*, filled their quivers with arrows, and the Jews from the quarter of la Xedrea did a rushing business, selling all their old iron, including lances, notched swords and rusty corselets, in exchange for good, ringing pieces of silver.

And off sped the Valencian galleys, with their jib-sails spread to the wind, convoyed by a shoal of dolphins, which sported about in the foam of their prows!... When the Moors beheld them approaching, the infidels began to tremble, repenting of their irreverence toward the Shrine. And this, despite the fact that they were a set of hardened old dogs. Valencians, headed by the valiant *blanquers*! Who, indeed, would dare face them!

The battle raged for several days and nights, according to the tale of Señor Vicente. Reinforcements of Moors arrived, but the Valencians, loyal and fierce, fought to the death. And they were already beginning to feel exhausted from the labor of disembowelling so many infidels, when behold, from a neighboring mountain a lion comes walking down on his hind paws, for all the world like a regular person, carrying in his forepaws, most reverently, the Shrine,—the Shrine that had been stolen from Torreblanca! The beast delivered it ceremoniously into the hands of one of the guild, undoubtedly an ancestor of Señor Vicente, and hence for centuries his family had possessed the privilege of representing that amiable animal in the Valencian processions.

Then he shook his mane, emitted a roar, and with blows and bites in every direction cleared the field instantly of Moors.

The Valencians sailed for home, carrying the Shrine back like a trophy. The chief of the *blanquers* saluted the lion, courteously offering him the guild house, near the towers of Serranos, which he could consider as his own. Many thanks; the beast was accustomed to the sun of Africa and feared a change of climate.

But the trade was not ungrateful, and to perpetuate the happy recollection of the shaggy-maned friend whom they possessed on the other shore of the sea, every time the guild banner floated in the Valencian celebrations, there marched behind it an ancestor of Señor Vicente, to the sound of drums, and he was covered with hide, with a mask that was the living image of the worthy lion, bearing in his hands a Shrine of wood, so small and poor that it caused one to doubt the genuine value of Torreblanca's own Shrine.

Perverse and irreverent persons even dared to affirm, to the great indignation of Señor Vicente, that the whole story was a lie. Sheer envy! Ill will of the other trades, which couldn't point to such a glorious history! There was the guild chapel as proof, and in it the lantern from the prow of the vessel, which the conscienceless wretches declared dated from many centuries after the supposed battle; and there were the guild drums, and the glorious banner; and the moth-eaten hide of the lion, in which all his predecessors had encased themselves, lay now forgotten behind the altar, covered with cobwebs and dust, but it was none the less as authentic and worthy of reverence as the stones of el Miguelete.[1]

And above all there was his faith, ardent and incontrovertible, capable of receiving as an affront to the family the slightest irreverence toward the African

---

1   A belfry in Valencia.

lion, the illustrious friend of the guild.

The procession took place on an afternoon in June. The sons, the daughters-in-law, and the grandsons of Señor Vicente helped him to get into the costume of the lion, perspiring most uncomfortably at the mere touch of that red-stained wool. "Father, you're going to roast."—"Grandpa, you'll melt inside of this costume."

The old man, however, deaf to the warnings of the family, shook his moth-eaten mane with pride, thinking of his ancestors; then he tried on the terrifying mask, a cardboard arrangement that imitated, with a faint resemblance, the countenance of the wild beast.

What a triumphant afternoon! The streets crowded with spectators; the balconies decorated with bunting, and upon them rows of variegated bonnets shading fair faces from the sun; the ground covered with myrtle, forming a green, odorous carpet whose perfume seemed to expand the lungs.

The procession was headed by the standard-bearers, with beards of hemp, crowns, and striped dalmatics, holding aloft the Valencian banners adorned with enormous bats and large L's beside the coat of arms; then, to the sound of the flageolet, the retinue of wild Indians, shepherds from Bethlehem, Catalans and Majorcans; following these passed the dwarfs with their monstrously huge heads, clicking the castanets to the rhythm of a Moorish march; behind these came the giants of the Corpus and at the end, the banners of the guilds; an endless row of red standards, faded with the years, and so tall that their tops reached higher than the first stories of the buildings.

Plom! Rotoplom! rolled the drums of the *blanquers*,—instruments of barbarous sonority, so large that their weight forced the drummers to bow their necks. Plom! Rotoplom! they resounded, hoarse and menacing, with savage solemnity, as if they were still marking the tread of the revolutionary guild regiments, sallying forth to the encounter with the emperor's young leader,—that Don Juan of Aragon, duke of Segorbe, who served Victor Hugo as the model for his romantic personage *Hernani*! Plom! Rotoplom! The people ran for good places and jostled one another to obtain a better view of the guild members, bursting into laughter and shouts. What was that? A monkey?... A wild man?... Ah! The faith of the past was truly laughable.

The young members of the trade, their shirts open at the neck and their sleeves rolled up, took turns at carrying the heavy banner, performing feats of jugglery, balancing it on the palms of their hands or upon their teeth, to the rhythm of the drums.

The wealthy masters had the honor of holding the cords of the banner, and behind them marched the lion, the glorious lion of the guild, who was now no longer known. Nor did the lion march in careless fashion; he was dignified, as the old traditions bade him be, and as Señor Vicente had seen his father march, and as the latter had seen his grandfather; he kept time with the drums, bowing at every step, to right and to left, moving the Shrine fan-wise, like a polite and well-bred beast who knows the respect due to the public.

The farmers who had come to the celebration opened their eyes in amazement; the mothers pointed him out with their fingers so that the children might see him; but the youngsters, frowning, tightened their grasp upon their mothers' necks, hiding their faces to shed tears of terror.

When the banner halted, the glorious lion had to defend himself with his hind paws against the disrespectful swarm of gamins that surrounded him, trying to tear some locks out of his moth-eaten mane. At other times the beast looked up at the balconies to salute the pretty girls with the Shrine; they laughed at the grotesque figure. And Señor Vicente did wisely; however much of a lion one may be, one must be gallant toward the fair sex.

The spectators fanned themselves, trying to find a momentary coolness in the burning atmosphere; the *horchateros*[2] bustled among the crowds shouting their wares, called from all directions at once and not knowing whither to go first; the standard-bearers and the drummers wiped the sweat off their faces at every restaurant door, and at last went inside to seek refreshment.

But the lion stuck to his post. His mask became soft; he walked with a certain weariness, letting the Shrine rest upon his stomach, having by this time lost all desire to bow to the public.

Fellow tanners approached him with jesting questions.

---

2   Vendors of "horchata," iced orgeat.

"How are things going, *so Visent*?"

And *so Visent* roared indignantly from the interior of his cardboard disguise. How should things go? Very well. He was able to keep it up, without failing in his part, even if the parade continued for three days. As for getting tired, leave that to the young folks. And drawing himself proudly erect, he resumed his bows, marking time with his swaying Shrine of wood.

The procession lasted three hours. When the guild banner returned to the Cathedral night was beginning to fall.

Plom! Retoplom! The glorious banner of the *blanquers* returned to its guild house behind the drums. The myrtle on the streets had disappeared beneath the feet of the paraders. Now the ground was covered with drops of wax, rose leaves and strips of tinsel. The liturgic perfume of incense floated through the air. Plom! Retoplom! The drums were tired; the strapping youths who had carried the standards were now panting, having lost all desire to perform balancing tricks; the rich masters clutched the cords of the banner tightly as if the latter were towing them along, and they complained of their new shoes and their bunions; but the lion, the weary lion (ah, swaggering beast!) who at times seemed on the point of falling to the ground, still had strength left to rise on his hind paws and frighten the suburban couples, who pulled at a string of children that had been dazzled by the sights.

A lie! Pure conceit! Señor Vicente knew what it felt like to be inside of the lion's hide. But nobody is obliged to take the part of the lion, and he who assumes it must stick it out to the bitter end.

Once home, he sank upon the sofa like a bundle of wool; his sons, daughters-in-law and grandchildren hastened to remove the mask from his face. They could scarcely recognize him, so congested and scarlet were his features, which seemed to spurt water from every line of his wrinkles.

They tried to remove his skins; but the beast was oppressed by a different desire, begging in a suffocated voice. He wished a drink; he was choking with the heat. The family, warning against illness, protested in vain. The deuce! He desired a drink right away. And who would dare resist an infuriated lion?...

From the nearest café they brought him some ice-cream in a blue cup; a Valencian ice-cream, honey-sweet and grateful to the nostrils, glistening with drops of white juice at the conical top.

But what are ice creams to a lion! *Haaam*! He swallowed it at a single gulp, as if it were a mere trifle! His thirst and the heat assailed him anew, and he roared for other refreshment.

The family, for reasons of economy, thought of the *horchata* from a near-by restaurant. They would see; let a full jar of it be brought. And Señor Vicente drank and drank until it was unnecessary to remove the skins from him. Why? Because an attack of double pneumonia finished him inside of a few hours. The glorious, shaggy-haired *uniform* of the family served him as a shroud.

Thus died the lion of the *blanquers*,—the last lion of Valencia.

And the fact is that *horchata* is fatal for beasts.... Pure poison!

THE TOAD

"I WAS spending the summer at Nazaret," said my friend Orduna, "a little fishermen's town near Valencia. The women went to the city to sell the fish, the men sailed about in their boats with triangular sails, or tugged at their nets on the beach; we summer vacationists spent the day sleeping and the night at the doors of our houses, contemplating the phosphorescence of the waves or slapping ourselves here and there whenever we heard the buzz of a mosquito,—that scourge of our resting hours.

"The doctor, a hardy and genial old fellow, would come and sit down under the bower before my door, and we'd spend the night together, with a jar or a watermelon at our side, speaking of his patients, folks of land or sea, credulous, rough and insolent in their manners, given over to fishing or to the cultivation of their fields. At times we laughed as he recalled the illness of Visanteta, the daughter of *la Soberana*, an old fishmonger who justified her nickname of *the Queen* by her bulk and her stature, as well as by the arrogance with which she treated her market companions, imposing her will upon them by right of might ... The belle of the place was this Visanteta: tiny, malicious, with a clever tongue, and no other good looks than that of youthful health; but she had a pair of penetrating eyes and a trick of pretending timidity, weakness, and interest, which simply turned the heads of the village youths. Her sweetheart was *Carafosca*, a brave fisherman who was capable of sailing on a stick of wood. On the sea he was admired by all for his audacity; on land he filled everybody with fear by his provoking silence and the facility with which he whipped out his aggressive sailor's knife. Ugly, burly, and always ready for a fight, like the huge creatures that from time to time showed up in the waters of Nazaret devouring all the fish, he would walk to church on Sunday afternoons at his sweetheart's side, and every time the maiden raised her head to speak to him, amidst the simple talk and lisping of a delicate, pampered child, *Carafosca* would cast a challenging look about him with his squinting eyes, as if defying all the folk of the fields, the beach, and the sea to take his Visanteta away from him.

"One day the most astounding news was bruited about Nazaret. The daughter of la *Soberana* had an animal inside of her. Her abdomen was swelling; the slow deformation revealed itself through her underskirts and her dress; her face lost color, and the fact that she had swooned several times, vomiting painfully, upset the entire cabin and caused her mother to burst into desperate lamentations and to run in terror for help. Many of her neighbors smiled when they heard of this illness. Let them tell it to *Carafosca*!... But the incredulous ones ceased their malicious talk and their suspicions when they saw how sad and desperate *Carafosca* became at his sweetheart's illness, praying for her recovery with all the fervor of a simple soul, even going so far as to enter the little village church,—

he, who had always been a pagan, a blasphemer of God and the saints.

"Yes, it was a strange and horrible sickness. The people, in their predisposition to believe in all sorts of extraordinary and rare afflictions, were certain that they knew what this was. Visanteta had a toad in her stomach. She had drunk from a certain spot of the near-by river, and the wicked animal, small and almost unnoticeable, had gone down into her stomach, growing fast. The good neighbors, trembling with stupefaction, flocked to *la Soberana's* cabin to examine the girl. All, with a certain solemnity, felt the swelling abdomen, seeking in its tightened surface the outlines of the hidden creature. Some of them, older and more experienced than the rest, laughed with a triumphant expression. There it was, right under their hand. They could feel it stirring, moving about.... Yes, it was moving! And after grave deliberation, they agreed upon remedies to expel the unwelcome guest. They gave the girl spoonfuls of rosemary honey, so that the wicked creature inside should start to eat it gluttonously, and when he was most preoccupied in his joyous meal, whiz!— an inundation of onion juice and vinegar that would bring him out at full gallop. At the same time they applied to her stomach miraculous plasters, so that the toad, left without a moment's rest, should escape in terror; there were rags soaked in brandy and saturated with incense; tangles of hemp dipped in the calking of the ships; mountain herbs; simple bits of paper with numbers, crosses and Solomon's seal upon them, sold by the miracle-worker of the city. Visanteta thought that all these remedies that were being thrust down her throat would be the death of her. She shuddered with the chills of nausea, she writhed in horrible contortions as if she were about to expel her very entrails, but the odious toad did not deign to show even one of his legs, and *la Soberana* cried to heaven. Ah, her daughter!... Those remedies would never succeed in casting out the wretched animal: it was better to let it alone, and not torture the poor girl; rather give it a great deal to eat, so that it wouldn't feed upon the strength of Visanteta who was growing paler and weaker every day.

"And as *la Soberana* was poor, all her friends, moved by the compassionate solidarity of the common people, devoted themselves to the feeding of Visanteta so that the toad should do her no harm. The fisher-women, upon returning from the square brought her cakes that were purchased in city establishments, that only the upper class patronized; on the beach, when the catch was sorted, they laid aside for her a dainty morsel that would serve for a succulent soup; the neighbors, who happened to be cooking in their pots over the fire would take out a cupful of the best of the broth, carrying it slowly so that it shouldn't spill, and bring it to *la Soberana's* cabin; cups of chocolate arrived one after the other every afternoon.

"Visanteta rebelled against this excessive kindness. She couldn't swallow another drop! She was full! But her mother stuck out her hairy nose with an imperious expression. I tell you to eat! She must remember what she had inside of her.... And she began to feel a faint, indefinable affection for that mysterious creature, lodged in the entrails of her daughter. She pictured it to herself; she could see it; it was her pride. Thanks to it, the whole town had its eyes upon the cabin and the trail of visitors was unending, and *la Soberana* never passed a woman on her way without being stopped and asked for news.

"Only once had they summoned the doctor, seeing him pass by the door; but not that they really wished him, or had any faith in him. What could that helpless man do against such a tenacious animal!... And upon hearing that, not content with the explanations of the mother and the daughter and his own audacious tapping around her clothes, he recommended an internal examination, the proud mother almost showed him the door. The impudent wretch! Not in a hurry was he going to have the pleasure of seeing her daughter so intimately! The poor thing, so good and so modest, who blushed merely at the thought of such proposals!...

"On Sunday afternoons Visanteta went to church, figuring at the head of the daughters of Mary. Her voluminous abdomen was eyed with admiration by the girls. They all asked breathlessly after the toad, and Visanteta replied wearily. It didn't bother her so much now. It had grown very much because she ate so well; sometimes it moved about, but it didn't hurt as it used to. One after the other the maidens would place their hands upon the afflicted one and feel the movements of the invisible creature, admiring as they did so the superiority of their friend. The curate, a blessed chap of pious simplicity, pretended not to notice the feminine curiosity, and thought with awe of the things done by God to put His creatures to the test. Afterwards, when the afternoon drew to a close, and the choir sang in gentle voice the praises of Our Lady of the Sea, each of the virgins would fall to thinking of that mysterious beast, praying fervently that poor Visanteta be delivered of it as soon as possible.

"*Carafosca*, too, enjoyed a certain notoriety because of his sweetheart's affliction. The women accosted him, the old fishermen stopped him to inquire about the animal that was torturing the girl. 'The poor thing! The poor thing!' he would groan, in accents of amorous commiseration. He said no more; but his eyes revealed a vehement desire to take over as soon as possible Visanteta and her toad, since the latter inspired a certain affection in him because of its connection with her.

"One night, when the doctor was at my door, a woman came in search of him, panting with dramatic horror. *La Soberana's* daughter was very sick; he must run to her rescue. The doctor shrugged his shoulders. 'Ah, yes! The toad!' And he didn't seem at all anxious to stir. Then came another woman, more agitated than the first. Poor Visanteta! She was dying! Her shrieks could be heard all over the street. The wicked beast was devouring her entrails....

"I followed the doctor, attracted by the curiosity that had the whole town in a commotion. When we came to *la Soberana's* cabin we had to force our way through a compact group of women who obstructed the doorway, crowding into the house. A rending shriek, a rasping wail came from the innermost part of the dwelling, rising above the heads of the curious or terrified women. The hoarse voice of *la Soberana* answered with entreating accents. Her daughter! Ah, Lord, her poor daughter....

"The arrival of the physician was received by a chorus of demands on the part of the old women. Poor Visanteta was writhing furiously, unable to bear such pain; her eyes bulged from their sockets and her features were distorted. She must be operated upon; her entrails must be opened and the green, slippery demon that was eating her alive must be expelled.

"The doctor proceeded upon his task, without paying any attention to the advice showered upon him, and before I could reach his side his voice resounded through the sudden silence, with ill-humored brusqueness:

"'But good Lord, the only trouble with this girl is that she's going to ...!'

"Before he could finish, all could guess from the harshness of his voice what he was about to say. The group of women yielded before *la Soberana's* thrusts even as the waves of the sea under the belly of a whale. She stuck out her big hands and her threatening nails, mumbling insults and looking at the doctor with murder in her eyes. Bandit! Drunkard! Out of her house!... It was the people's fault, for supporting such an infidel.

She'd eat him up! Let them make way for her!... And she struggled violently with her friends, fighting to free herself and scratch out the doctor's eyes. To her vindictive cries were joined the weak bleating of Visanteta, protesting with the breath that was left her between her groans of pain. It was a lie! Let that wicked man be gone! What a nasty mouth he had! It was all a lie!...

"But the doctor went hither and thither, asking for water, for bandages, snappy and imperious in his commands, paying no attention whatsoever to the threats of the mother or the cries of the daughter, which were becoming louder and more heart-rending than ever. Suddenly she roared as if she were being slaughtered, and there was a bustle of curiosity around the physician, whom I couldn't see. 'It's a lie! A lie! Evil-tongued wretch! Slanderer!' ... But the protestations of Visanteta were no longer unaccompanied. To her voice of an innocent victim begging justice from heaven was added the cry of a pair of lungs that were breathing the air for the first time.

"And now the friends of *la Soberana* had to restrain her from falling upon her daughter. She would kill her! The bitch! Whose child was that?... And terrified by the threats of her mother, the sick woman, who was still sobbing 'It's a lie! A lie!' at last spoke. It was a young fellow of the *huerta* whom she had never seen again ... an indiscretion committed one evening.... She no longer remembered. No, she could not remember!... And she insisted upon this forgetfulness as if it were an incontrovertible excuse.

"The people now saw through it all. The women were impatient to spread the news. As we left, *la Soberana*, humiliated and in tears, tried to kneel before the doctor and kiss his hand. 'Ay, Don Antoni!... Don Antoni!' She asked pardon for her insults; she despaired when she thought of the village comments. What they would have to suffer now!... On the following day the youths that sang as they arranged their nets would invent new verses. The song of the toad! Her life would become impossible!... But even more than this, the thought of *Carafosca* terrified her. She knew very well what sort of brute that was. He would kill poor Visanteta the first time she appeared on the street; and she herself would meet the same fate for being her mother and not having guarded her well. 'Ay, Don Antoni!' She begged him, upon her knees, to see *Carafosca*. He, who was so good and who knew so much, could convince the fellow with his reasoning, and make him swear that he would not do the women any harm,—that he would forget them.

"The doctor received these entreaties with the same indifference as he had received the threats, and he answered sharply. He would see about it; it was a delicate affair. But once in the street, he shrugged his shoulders with resignation. 'Let's go and see that animal.'

"We pulled him out of the tavern and the three of us began to walk along the beach through the darkness. The fisherman seemed to be awed at finding himself between two persons of such importance. Don Antonio spoke to him of the indisputable superiority of men ever since the earliest days of creation; of the scorn with which women should be regarded because of their lack of seriousness; of their immense number and the ease with which we could pick another if the one we had happened to displease us ... and at last, with brutal directness, told what had happened.

"*Carafosca* hesitated, as if he had not understood the doctor's words very well. Little by little the certainty dawned upon his dense comprehension. 'By God! By God!' And he scratched himself fearfully under his cap, and brought his hands to his sash as if he were seeking his redoubtable knife.

"The physician tried to console him. He must forget Visanteta; there would be no sense or advantage in killing her. It wasn't worth while for a splendid chap like him to go to prison for slaying a worthless creature like her. The real culprit was that unknown laborer; but ... and she! And how easily she ... committed the indiscretion, not being able to recall anything afterwards!...

"For a long time we walked along in painful silence, with no other novelty than *Carafosca's* scratching of his head and his sash. Suddenly he surprised us with the roar of his voice, speaking to us in Castilian, thus adding solemnity to what he said:

"'Do you want me to tell you something?... Do you want me to tell you something?'

"He looked at us with hostile eyes, as if he saw before him the unknown culprit of the *huerta*, ready to pounce upon him. It could be seen that his sluggish brain had just adopted a very firm resolution.... What was it? Let him speak.

"'Well, then,' he articulated slowly, as if we were enemies whom he desired to confound, 'I tell you ... that now I love the girl more than ever.'

"In our stupefaction, at a loss for reply, we shook hands with him."

COMPASSION

AT TEN o'clock in the evening Count de Sagreda walked into his club on the Boulevard des Capucins. There was a bustle among the servants to relieve him of his cane, his highly polished hat and his costly fur coat, which, as it left his shoulders revealed a shirt bosom of immaculate neatness, a gardenia in his lapel, and all the attire of black and white, dignified yet brilliant, that belongs to a gentleman who has just dined.

The story of his ruin was known by every member of the club. His fortune, which fifteen years before had caused a certain commotion in Paris, having been ostentatiously cast to the four winds, was exhausted. The count was now living on the remains of his opulence, like those shipwrecked seamen who live upon the debris of the vessel, postponing in anguish the arrival of the last hour. The very servants who danced attendance upon him like slaves in dress suits, knew of his misfortune and discussed his shameful plight; but not even the slightest suggestion of insolence disturbed the colorless glance of their eyes, petrified by servitude. He was such a nobleman! He had scattered his money with such majesty!... Besides, he was a genuine member of the nobility, a nobility that dated back for centuries and whose musty odor inspired a certain ceremonious gravity in many of the citizens whose forebears had helped bring about the Revolution. He was not one of those Polish counts who permit themselves to be entertained by women, nor an Italian marquis who winds up by cheating at cards, nor a Russian personage of consequence who often draws his pay from the police; he was genuine *hidalgo*, a grandee of Spain. Perhaps one of his ancestors figured in the *Cid*, in *Ruy Blas* or some other of the heroic pieces in the repertory of the Comédie Française.

The count entered the salons of the club with head erect and a proud gait, greeting his friends with a barely discernible smile, a mixture of hauteur and light-heartedness.

He was approaching his fortieth year, but he was still the *beau* Sagreda, as he had long been nicknamed by the noctambulous women of Maxim's and the early-rising Amazons of the Bois. A few gray hairs at his temples and a triangle of faint wrinkles at the corner of his brows, betrayed the effects of an existence that had been lived at too rapid a pace, with the vital machinery running at full speed. But his eyes were still youthful, intense and melancholy; eyes that caused him to be called "the Moor" by his men and women friends. The Viscounte de la Tresminière, crowned by the Academy as the author of a study on one of his ancestors who had been a companion of Condé, and highly appreciated by the antique dealers on the left bank of the Seine, who sold him all the bad canvases they had in store, called him *Velazquez*, satisfied that the swarthy, somewhat olive complexion of the count, his black, heavy mustache and his grave eyes, gave him the right to display his thorough acquaintance with Spanish art.

All the members of the club spoke of Sagreda's ruin with discreet compassion. The poor count! Not to fall heir to some new legacy. Not to meet some American millionairess who would be smitten with him and his titles!... They must do something to save him.

And he walked amid this mute and smiling pity without being at all aware of it, encased in his pride, receiving as admiration that which was really compassionate sympathy, forced to have recourse to painful simulations in order to surround himself with as much luxury as before, thinking that he was deceiving others and deceiving only himself.

Sagreda cherished no illusions as to the future. All the relatives that might come to his rescue with a timely legacy had done so many years before, upon making their exit from the world's stage. None that might recall his name was left beyond the mountains. In Spain he had only some distant relatives, personages of the nobility united to him more by historic bonds than by ties of blood. They addressed him familiarly, but he could expect from them no help other than good advice and admonitions against his wild extravagance ... It was all over. Fifteen years of dazzling display had consumed the supply of wealth with which Sagreda one day arrived in Paris. The granges of Andalusia, with their droves of cattle and horses, had changed hands without ever having made the acquaintance of this owner, devoted to luxury and always absent. After them, the vast wheat fields of Castilla and the rice fields of Valencia, and the villages of the northern provinces, had gone into strange hands,—all the princely possessions of the ancient counts of Sagreda, plus the inheritances from various pious aunts, and the considerable legacies of other relatives who had died of old age in their ancient country houses.

Paris and the elegant summer seasons had in a few years devoured this fortune of centuries. The recollection of a few noisy love affairs with two actresses in vogue; the nostalgic smile of a dozen costly women of the world; the forgotten fame of several duels; a certain prestige as a rash, calm gambler, and a reputation as a knightly swordsman, intransigeant in matters of honor, were all that remained to the *beau* Sagreda after his downfall.

He lived upon his past, contracting new debts with certain providers who, recalling other financial crises, trusted to a re-establishment of his fortune. "His fate was settled," according to the count's own words. When he could do no more, he would resort to a final course. Kill himself?... never. Men like him committed suicide only because of gambling debts or debts of honor. Ancestors of his, noble and glorious, had owed huge sums to persons who were not their equals, without for a moment considering suicide on this account. When the creditors should shut their doors to him, and the money-lenders should threaten him with a public court scandal, Count de Sagreda, making a heroic effort, would wrench himself away from the sweet Parisian life. His ancestors had been soldiers and colonizers. He would join the foreign legion of Algeria, or would take passage for that America which had been conquered by his forefathers, becoming a mounted shepherd in the solitudes of Southern Chile or upon the boundless plains of Patagonia.

Until the dreaded moment should arrive, this hazardous, cruel existence that forced him to live a continuous lie, was the best period of his career. From his last trip to Spain, made for the purpose of liquidating certain remnants of his patrimony, he had returned with a woman, a maiden of the provinces who had been captivated by the prestige of the nobleman; in her affection, ardent and submissive at the same time, there was almost as much admiration as love. A woman!... Sagreda for the first time realized the full significance of this word, as if up to then he had not understood it. His present companion was a woman; the nervous, dissatisfied females who had filled his previous existence, with their painted smiles and voluptuous artifices, belonged to another species.

And now that the real woman had arrived, his money was departing forever!... And when misfortune appeared, love came with it!... Sagreda, lamenting his lost fortune, struggled hard to maintain his outward pompous show. He lived as before, in the same house, without retrenching his budget, making his companion presents of value equal to those that he had lavished upon his former women friends, enjoying an almost paternal satisfaction before the childish surprise and the ingenuous happiness of the poor girl, who was overwhelmed by the brilliant life of Paris.

Sagreda was drowning,—drowning!—but with a smile on his lips, content with himself, with his present life, with this sweet dream, which was to be the final one and which was lasting miraculously long. Fate, which had maltreated him in the past few years, consuming the remainders of his wealth at Monte Carlo, at Ostend and in the notable clubs of the Boulevard, seemed now to stretch out a helping hand, touched by his new existence. Every night, after dining with his companion at a fashionable restaurant, he would leave her at the theatre and go to his club, the only place where luck awaited him. He did not plunge heavily. Simple games of écarté with intimate friends, chums of his youth, who continued their happy career with the aid of great fortunes, or who had settled down after marrying wealth, retaining among their former habits the custom of visiting the honorable circle.

Scarcely did the count take his seat, with his cards in his hand, opposite one of these friends, when Fortune seemed to hover over his head, and his friends did not tire of playing, inviting him to a game every night, as if they stood awaiting their turn. His winnings were hardly enough to grow wealthy upon; some nights ten *louis*; others twenty-five; on special occasions Sagreda would retire with as many as forty gold coins in his pocket. But thanks to this almost daily gain he was able to fill the gaps of his lordly existence, which threatened to topple down upon his head, and he maintained his lady companion in surroundings of loving comfort, at the same time recovering confidence in his immediate future. Who could tell what was in store for him?...

Noticing Viscount de la Tresminière in one of the salons he smiled at him with an expression of friendly challenge.

"What do you say to a game?"

"As you wish, my dear *Velazquez*."

"Seven francs per five points will be sufficient. I'm sure to win. Luck is with me."

"Seven francs per five points will be sufficient. I'm sure to win. Luck is with me."

The game commenced under the soft light of the electric bulbs, amid the soothing silence of soft carpets and thick curtains.

Sagreda kept winning, as if his kind fate was pleased to extricate him from the most difficult passes. He won without half trying. It made no difference that he lacked trumps and that he held bad cards; those of his rival were always worse, and the result would be miraculously in harmony with his previous games.

Already, twenty-five golden *louis* lay before him. A club companion, who was wandering from one salon to the other with a bored expression, stopped near the players interested in the game. At first he remained standing near Sagreda; then he took up his position behind the viscount, who seemed to be rendered nervous and perturbed at the fellow's proximity.

"But that's awfully silly of you!" the inquisitive newcomer soon exclaimed. "You're not playing a good game, my dear viscount. You're laying aside your trumps and using only your bad cards. How stupid of you!"

He could say no more. Sagreda threw his cards upon the table. He had grown terribly white, with a greenish pallor. His eyes, opened extraordinarily wide, stared at the viscount. Then he rose.

"I understand," he said coldly. "Allow me to withdraw."

Then, with a quivering hand, he thrust the heap of gold coins toward his friend.

"This belongs to you."

"But, my dear *Velasquez* ... Why, Sagreda!... Permit me to explain, dear count!..."

"Enough, sir. I repeat that I understand."

His eyes flashed with a strange gleam, the selfsame gleam that his friends had seen upon various occasions, when after a brief dispute or an insulting word, he raised his glove in a gesture of challenge.

But this hostile glance lasted only a moment. Then he smiled with glacial affability.

"Many thanks, Viscount. These are favors that are never forgotten ... I repeat my gratitude."

And he saluted, like a true noble, walking off proudly erect, the same as in the most smiling days of his opulence.

* * * *

With his fur coat open, displaying his immaculate shirt bosom, Count de Sagreda promenades along the boulevard. The crowds are issuing from the theatres; the women are crossing from one sidewalk to the other; automobiles with lighted interiors roll by, affording a momentary glimpse of plumes, jewels and white bosoms; the news-vendors shout their wares; at the top of the buildings huge electrical advertisements blaze forth and go out in rapid succession.

The Spanish grandee, the *hidalgo*, the descendant of the noble knights of the *Cid* and *Ruy Blas*, walks against the current, elbowing his way through the crowd, desiring to hasten as fast as possible, without any particular objective in view.

To contract debts!... Very well. Debts do not dishonor a nobleman. But to receive alms?... seeing his friends desert him, of descending to the lowest depths, being lost in the social substratum. But to arouse compassion....

The comedy was useless. The intimate friends who smiled at him in former times had penetrated the secret of his poverty and had been moved by pity to get together and take turns at giving him alms under the pretext of gambling with him. And likewise his other friends, and even the servants who bowed to him with their accustomed respect as he passed by, were in the secret. And he, the poor dope, was going about with his lordly airs, stiff and solemn in his extinct grandeur, like the corpse of the legendary chieftain, which, after his death, was mounted on horseback and sallied forth to win battles.

Farewell, Count de Sagreda! The heir of governors and viceroys can become a nameless soldier in a legion of desperadoes and bandits; he can begin life anew as an adventurer in virgin lands, killing that he may live;

he can even watch with impassive countenance the wreck of his name and his family history, before the bench of a tribunal ... But to live upon the compassion of his friends!...

Farewell forever, final illusions! The count has forgotten his companion, who is waiting for him at a night restaurant. He does not think of her; it is as if he never had seen her; as if she had never existed. He thinks not at all of that which but a few hours before had made life worth living. He walks along, alone with his disgrace, and each step of his seems to draw from the earth a dead thing; an ancestral influence, a racial prejudice, a family boast, dormant hauteur, honor and fierce pride, and as these awake, they oppress his breast and cloud his thoughts.

How they must have laughed at him behind his back, with condescending pity!... Now he walks along more hurriedly than ever, as if he has at last made up his mind just where he is going, and his emotion leads him unconsciously to murmur with irony, as if he is speaking to somebody who is at his heels and whom he desires to flee.

"Many thanks! Many thanks!"

Just before dawn two revolver shots astound the guests of a hotel in the vicinity of the *Gare Saint-Lazare*,—one of those ambiguous establishments that offers a safe shelter for amorous acquaintances begun on the thoroughfare.

The attendants find in one of the rooms a gentleman dressed in evening clothes, with a hole in his head, through which escape bloody strips of flesh. The man writhes like a worm upon the threadbare carpet.

His eyes, of a dull black, still glitter with life. There is nothing left in them of the image of his sweet companion. His last thought, interrupted by death, is of friendship, terrible in its pity; of the fraternal insult of a generous, light-hearted compassion.

THE WINDFALL

"I, SIR," said *Magdalena*, the bugler of the prison, "am no saint; I've been jailed many times for robberies; some of them that really took place and others that I was simply suspected of. Compared to you, who are a gentleman, and are in prison for having written things in the papers, I'm a mere wretch ... But take my word for it, this time I'm here for good."

And raising one hand to his breast as he straightened his head with a certain pride, he added, "Petty thefts, that's all ... I'm not brave; I haven't shed a drop of blood."

At break of day, *Magdalena's* bugle resounded through the spacious yard, embroidering its reveille with scales and trills. During the day, with the martial instrument hanging from his neck, or caressing it with a corner of his smock so as to wipe off the vapor with which the dampness of the prison covered it, he would go through the entire edifice,—an ancient convent in whose refectories, granaries, and garrets there were crowded, in perspiring confusion, almost a thousand men.

He was the clock that governed the life and the activities of this mass of male flesh perpetually seething with hatred. He made the round of the cells to announce, with sonorous blasts, the arrival of the worthy director, or a visit from the authorities; from the progress of the sun along the white walls of the prison-yard he could tell the approach of the visiting hours,—the best part of the day,—and with his tongue stuck between his lips he would await orders impatiently, ready to burst into the joyous signal that sent the flock of prisoners scampering over the stairways in an anxious run toward the locutories, where a wretched crowd of women and children buzzed in conversation; his insatiable hunger kept him pacing back and forth in the vicinity of the old kitchen, in which the enormous stews filled the atmosphere with a nauseating odor, and he bemoaned the indifference of the chef, who was always late in giving the order for the mess-call.

Those imprisoned for crimes of blood, heroes of the dagger who had killed their man in a fierce brawl or in a dispute over a woman and who formed an aristocracy that disdained the petty thieves, looked upon the bugler as the butt for pranks with which to while away their boredom.

"Blow!" would come the command from some formidable fellow, proud of his crimes and his courage.

And *Magdalena* would draw himself up with military rigidity, close his mouth and inflate his cheeks, momentarily expecting two blows, delivered simultaneously by both hands, to expel the air from the ruddy globe of his face. At other times these redoubtable personages tested the strength of their arms upon *Magdalena's* pate, which was bare with the baldness of repugnant diseases, and they would howl with laughter at the damage done to their fists by the protuberances of the hard skull. The bugler lent himself to these tortures with the humility of a whipped dog, and found a certain revenge in repeating, afterwards, those words that were a solace to him:

"I'm good; I'm not a brave fellow. Petty thefts, that's all ... But as to blood, not a single drop."

Visiting time brought his wife, the notorious *Peluchona*, a valiant creature who inspired him with great fear. She was the mistress of one of the most dangerous bandits in the jail. Daily she brought that fellow food, procuring these dainties at the cost of all manner of vile labors. The bugler, upon beholding her, would leave the lucutory, fearing the arrogance of her bandit mate, who would take advantage of the occasion to humiliate him before his former companion. Many times a certain feeling of curiosity and tenderness got the better of his fear, and he would advance timidly, looking beyond the thick bars for the head of a child that came with *la Peluchona*.

"That's my son, sir," he said humbly. "My Tonico, who no longer knows me or remembers me. They say that he doesn't resemble me at all. Perhaps he's not mine.... You can imagine, with the life his mother has always led, living near the garrisons, washing the soldiers' clothes!... But he was born in my home; I held him in my arms when he was ill, and that's a bond as close as ties of blood."

Then he would resume his timid lurking about the locutory, as if preparing one of his robberies, to see his Tonico; and when he could see him for a moment, the sight was enough to extinguish his helpless rage before the full basket of lunch that the evil woman brought to her lover.

Magdalena's whole existence was summed up in two facts; he had robbed and he had travelled much. The robberies were insignificant; clothes or money snatched in the street, because he lacked courage for greater deeds. His travels had been compulsory,— always on foot, over the roads of Spain, marching in a chain gang of convicts, between the polished or white three-cornered hats that guarded the prisoners.

After having been a "pupil" among the buglers of a regiment, he had launched upon his life of continuous imprisonment, punctuated by brief periods of freedom, in which he lost his bearings, not knowing what to do with himself and wishing to return as soon as possible to jail. It was the perpetual chain, but finished link by link, as he used to say.

The police never organized a round-up of dangerous persons but what *Magdalena* was found among them,—a timorous rat whose name the papers mentioned like that of a terrible criminal. He was always included in the trail of vagrant suspects who, without being charged with any specific crime, were sent from province to province by the authorities, in the hope that they would die of hunger along the roads, and thus he had covered the whole peninsula on foot, from Cádiz to Santander, from Valencia to La Coruna. With what enthusiasm he recalled his travels! He spoke of them as if they were joyous excursions, just like a wandering charity-student of the old *Tuna* converting his tales into courses in picturesque geography. With hungry delight he recollected the abundant milk of Galicia, the red sausages of Extramadura, the Castilian bread, the Basque apples, the wines and ciders of all the districts he had traversed, with his luggage on his shoulder. Guards were changed every day,—some of them kind or indifferent, others ill-humored and cruel, who made all the prisoners fear a couple of shots fired beyond the ruts of the road, followed by the papers justifying the killing as having been caused by an attempt at flight. With a certain nostalgia he evoked the memory of mountains covered with snow or reddened and striped by the sun; the slow procession along the white road that was lost in the horizon, like an endless ribbon; the highlands, under the trees, in the hot noon hours; the storms that assailed them upon the highways; inundated ravines that forced them to camp out in the open; the arrival, late at night, at certain town prisons, old convents or abandoned churches, in which every man hunted up a dry corner, protected from draughts, where he could stretch his mat; the endless journey with all the long halts in spots where life was so monotonous that the presence of a group of prisoners was an event; the urchins would come running up to the bars to speak with them, while the girls, impelled by morbid curiosity, would approach within a short distance, to hear their songs and their obscene language.

"Some mighty interesting travels, sir," continued the robber. "For those of us who had good health and didn't drop by the roadside it was the same as a strolling band of students. Now and then a drubbing, but who pays any attention to such things!... They don't have these *conductions* now; prisoners are transported by railroad, caged up in the cars. Besides I am held for a criminal offense, and I must live inside the walls ... jailed for good."

And again he began to lament his bad luck, relating the final deed that had landed him in jail.

It was a suffocating Sunday in July; an afternoon in which the streets of Valencia seemed to be deserted, under the burning sun and a wind like a furnace blast that came from the baked plains of the interior. Everybody was at the bull-fight or at the sea-shore. *Magdalena* was approached by his friend *Chamorra*, an old prison traveling companion, who exercised a certain influence over him. That *Chamorra* was a bad soul! A thief, but of the sort that go the limit, not recoiling before the necessity of shedding blood and with his knife always handy beside his skeleton-keys. It was a matter of cleaning out a certain house, upon which this fearful fellow had set his eye. *Magdalena* modestly excused himself. He wasn't made for such things; he couldn't go so far. As for gliding up to a roof and pulling down the clothes that had been hung out to dry, or snatching a woman's purse with a quick pull and making off with it ... all right. But to break into a house, and face the mystery of a dwelling, in which the people might be at home?...

But *Chamorra's* threatening look inspired him

with greater fear than did the anticipation of such an encounter, and he finally consented. Very well; he would go as an assistant,—to carry the spoils, but ready to flee at the slightest alarm. And he refused to accept an old jack-knife that his companion offered him. He was consistent.

"Petty thefts aplenty; but as to blood, not a single drop."

Late in the afternoon they entered the narrow vestibule of a house that had no janitor, and whose inhabitants were all away. *Chamorra* knew his victim; a comfortably fixed artisan who must have a neat little pile saved up. He was surely at the beach with his wife or at the bull-fight. Above, the door of the apartment yielded easily, and the two companions began to work in the gloom of the shuttered windows.

Chamorra forced the locks of two chiffoniers and a closet. There was silver coin, copper coin, several bank-notes rolled up at the bottom of a fan-case, the wedding-jewelry, a clock. Not a bad haul. His anxious looks wandered over the place, seeking to make off with everything that could be carried. He lamented the uselessness of *Magdalena*, who, restless with fear and with his arms hanging limp at his sides, was pacing to and fro without knowing what to do.

"Take the quilts," ordered *Chamorra*, "we're sure to get something for the wool." And *Magdalena*, eager to finish the job as soon as possible, penetrated into the dark alcove, gropingly passing a rope underneath the quilts and the bed-sheets. Then, aided by his friend, he hurriedly made a bundle of everything, casting the voluminous burden upon his shoulders.

They left without being detected, and walked off in the direction of the outskirts of the town, toward a shanty of Arrancapinos, where *Chamorra* had his haunt. The latter walked ahead, ready to run at the first sign of danger; *Magdalena* followed, trotting along, almost hidden beneath the tremendous load, fearing to feel at any moment the hand of the police upon his neck.

Upon examining the proceeds of the robbery in the remote corral, *Chamorra* exhibited the arrogance of a lion, granting his accomplice a few copper coins. This must be enough for the moment. He did this for *Magdalena's* own good, as *Magdalena* was such a spendthrift. Later he would give more.

Then they untied the bundle of quilts, and *Chamorra* bent over, his hands on his hips, exploding with laughter. What a find!... What a present!

Magdalena likewise burst into guffaws, for the first time that afternoon. Upon the bed-clothes lay an infant, dressed only in a little shirt, its eyes shut and its face purple from suffocation, but moving its chest with difficulty at feeling the first caress of fresh air. *Magdalena* recalled the vague sensation he had experienced during his journey hither,—that of something alive moving inside the thick load on his back. A weak, suffocated whining pursued him in his flight.... The mother had left the little one asleep in the cool darkness of the alcove, and they, without knowing it, had carried it off together with the bed-clothes.

Magdalena's frightened eyes now looked questioningly at his companion. What were they to do with the child?... But that evil soul was laughing away like a very demon.

"It's yours; I present it to you.... Eat it with potatoes."

And he went off with all the spoils. *Magdalena* was left standing in doubt, while he cradled the child in his arms. The poor little thing!... It looked just like his own Tono, when he was ill and leaned his little head upon his father's bosom, while the parent wept, fearing for the child's life. The same little soft, pink feet; the same downy flesh, with skin as soft as silk.... The infant had ceased to cry, looking with surprised eyes at the robber, who was caressing it like a nurse.

"Lullaby, my poor little thing! There, there, my little king ... child Jesus! Look at me. I'm your uncle."

But *Magdalena* stopped laughing, thinking of the mother, of her desperate grief when she would return to the house. The loss of her little fortune would be her least concern. The child! Where was she to find her child?... He knew what mothers were like. *Peluchona* was the worst of women, yet he had seen even her weep and moan before her little one in danger.

He gazed toward the sun, which was beginning to sink in a majestic summer sunset. There was still time to take the infant back to the house before its parents would return. And if he should encounter them, he would lie, saying that he found the infant in the middle of the street; he would extricate himself as well as he could. Forward; he had never felt so brave.

Carrying the infant in his arms he walked at ease through the very streets over which he had lately hastened with the anxious gait of fear. He mounted the staircase without encountering anybody. Above, the same solitude. The door was still open, the bolt forced. Within, the disordered rooms, the broken furniture, the drawers upon the floor, the overturned chairs and clothes strewn about, filled him with a sensation of terror similar to that which assails the assassin who returns to contemplate the corpse of his victim some time after the crime.

He gave a last fond kiss to the child and left it upon the bed.

"Good-bye, my pet!"

But as he approached the head of the staircase he heard footsteps, and in the rectangle of light that entered through the open door there bulked the silhouette of a corpulent man. At the same time there rang out the shrill shriek of a female voice, trembling with fright:

"Robbers!... Help!"

Magdalena tried to escape, opening a passage for himself with his head lowered, like a cornered rat; but he felt himself seized by a pair of Cyclopean arms, accustomed to beating iron, and with a mighty thrust he was sent rolling down the stairs.

On his face there were still signs of the bruises he had received from contact with the steps, and from the blows rained upon him by the infuriated neighbors.

"In sum, sir. Breaking and entering. I'll get out in heaven knows how many years ... All for being kind-hearted. To make matters worse, they don't even give me any consideration, looking upon me as a clever criminal. Everybody knows that the real thief was *Chamorra* whom I haven't seen since.... And they ridicule me for a silly fool."

LUXURY

"I HAD her on my lap," said my friend Martinez, "and the warm weight of her healthy body was beginning to tire me.

"The scene ... same as usual in such places. Mirrors with blemished surfaces, and names scratched across them, like spiders' webs; sofas of discolored velvet, with springs that creaked atrociously; the bed decorated with theatrical hangings, as clean and common as a sidewalk, and on the walls, pictures of bull-fighters and cheap chromos of angelic virgins smelling a rose or languorously contemplating a bold hunter.

"The scenery was that of the favorite cell in the convent of vice; an elegant room reserved for distinguished patrons; and she was a healthy, robust creature, who seemed to bring a whiff of the pure mountain air into the heavy atmosphere of this closed house, saturated with cheap cologne, rice powder and the vapor from dirty wash-basins.

"As she spoke to me she stroked the ribbons of her gown with childish complacency; it was a fine piece of satin, of screaming yellow, somewhat too tight for her body, a dress which I recalled having seen months before on the delicate charms of another girl, who had since died, according to reports, in the hospital.

"Poor girl! She had become a sight! Her coarse, abundant hair, combed in Greek fashion, was adorned with glass beads; her cheeks, shiny from the dew of perspiration, were covered with a thick layer of cosmetic; and as if to reveal her origin, her arms, which were firm, swarthy and of masculine proportions, escaped from the ample sleeves of her chorus-girl costume.

"As she saw me follow with attentive glance all the details of her extravagant array, she thought that I was admiring her, and threw her head back with a petulant expression.

"And such a simple creature!... She hadn't yet become acquainted with the customs of the house, and told the truth,—all the truth—to the men who wished to know her history. They called her Flora; but her real name was Mari-Pepa. She wasn't the orphan of a colonel or a magistrate, nor did she concoct the complicated tales of love and adventure that her companions did, in order to justify their presence in such a place. The truth; always the truth; she would yet be hanged for her frankness. Her parents were comfortably situated farmers in a little town of Aragón; owned their fields, had two mules in the barn, bread, wine, and enough potatoes for the year round; and at night the best fellows in the place came one after the other to soften her heart with serenade upon serenade, trying to carry off her dark, healthy person together with the four orchards she had inherited from her grandfather.

"'But what could you expect, my dear fellow?... I couldn't bear those people. They were too coarse for me. I was born to be a lady. And tell me, why can't I be? Don't I look as good as any of them?...'

"And she snuggled her head against my shoulder,

like the docile sweetheart she was,—a slave subjected to all sorts of caprices in exchange for being clothed handsomely.

"'Those fellows,' she continued, 'made me sick. I ran off with the student,—understand?—the son of the town magistrate, and we wandered about until he deserted me, and I landed here, waiting for something better to turn up. You see, it's a short tale ... I don't complain of anything. I'm satisfied.'

"And to show how happy she was, the unhappy girl rode astride my legs, thrust her hard fingers through my hair, rumpling it, and sang a tango in horrible fashion, in her strong, peasant voice.

"I confess that I was seized with an impulse to speak to her 'in the name of morality,'—that hypocritical desire we all possess to propagate virtue when we are sated and desire is dead.

"She raised her eyes, astonished to see me look so solemn, preaching to her, like a missionary glorifying chastity with a prostitute on his knees; her gaze wandered continually from my austere countenance to the bed close by. Her common sense was baffled before the incongruity between such virtue and the excesses of a moment before.

"Suddenly she seemed to understand, and an outburst of laughter swelled her fleshy neck."

"'The deuce!... How amusing you are! And with what a face you say all these things! Just like the priest of my home town ...'

"No, Pepa, I'm serious. I believe you're a good

girl; you don't realize what you've gone into, and I'm warning you. You've fallen very low, very low. You're at the bottom. Even within the career of vice, the majority of women resist and deny the caresses that are required of you in this house. There is yet time for you to save yourself. Your parents have enough for you to live on; you didn't come here under the necessity of poverty. Return to your home, and the past will be forgotten; you can tell them a lie, invent some sort of tale to justify your flight, and who knows?... One of the fellows that used to serenade you will marry you, you'll have children and you'll be a respectable woman.

"The girl became serious when she saw that I was speaking in earnest. Little by little she began to slip from my knees until she was on her feet, eyeing me fixedly, as if she saw before her some strange person and an invisible wall had arisen between the two.

"'Go back to my home!' she exclaimed in harsh accents. 'Many thanks. I know very well what that means. Get up before dawn, work like a slave, go out in the fields, ruin your hands with callouses. Look, see how my hands still show them.'

"And she made me feel the rough lumps that rose on the palms of her strong hands.

"'And all this, in exchange for what? For being respectable?... Not a bit of it! I'm not that crazy. So much for respectability!'

"And she accompanied these words with some indecent motions that she had picked up from her companions.

"Afterwards, humming a tune, she went over to the mirror to survey herself, and smilingly greeted the reflection of her powdered hair, covered with false pearls, which shone out of the cracked mirror. She contracted her lips, which were rouged like those of a clown.

"Growing more and more firm in my virtuous rôle, I continued to sermonize her from my chair, enveloping this hypocritical propaganda in sonorous words. She was making a bad choice; she must think of the future. The present could not be worse. What was she? Less than a slave; a piece of furniture; they exploited her, they robbed her, and afterwards ... afterwards it would be still worse; the hospital, repulsive diseases ...

"But again her harsh laughter interrupted me.

"'Quit it, boy. Don't bother me.'

"And planting herself before me she wrapped me in a gaze of infinite compassion.

"'Why my dear fellow, how silly you are! Do you imagine that I can go back to that dog's life, after having tasted this one?... No, sir! I was born for luxury.'

"And, with devoted admiration sweeping her glance across the broken chairs, the faded sofa, and that bed which was a public thoroughfare, she began to walk up and down, revelling in the rustle of her train as it dragged across the room, and caressing the folds of that gown which seemed to preserve the warmth of the other girl's body."

RABIES

FROM all the countryside the neighbors of the *huerta* flocked to *Caldera's* cabin, entering it with a certain meekness, a mingling of emotion and fear.

How was the boy? Was he improving?... Uncle Pascal, surrounded by his wife, his daughters-in-law and even the most distant relatives, who had been gathered together by misfortune, received with melancholy satisfaction this interest of the entire vicinity in the health of his son. Yes, he was getting better. For two days he had not been attacked by that horrible *thing* which set the cabin in commotion. And *Caldera's* laconic farmer friends, as well as the women, who were vociferous in the expression of their emotions, appeared at the threshold of the room, asking timidly, "How do you feel?"

The only son of *Caldera* was in there, sometimes in bed, in obedience to his mother, who could conceive of no illness without the cup of hot water and seclusion between the bed-sheets; at other times he sat up, his jaws supported by his hands, gazing obstinately into the furthermost corner of the room. His father, wrinkling his shaggy white brows, would walk about when left alone, or, through force of habit, take a look at the neighboring fields, but without any desire to bend over and pluck out any of the weeds that were beginning to sprout in the furrows. Much this land mattered to him now,—the earth in whose bowels he had left the sweat of his body and the strength of his limbs!... His son was all he had,—the fruit of a late marriage,—and he was a sturdy youth, as industrious and taciturn as his father; a soldier of the soil, who required neither orders nor threat to fulfil his duties; ready to awake at midnight when it was his turn to irrigate his land and give the fields drink under the light of the stars; quick to spring from his bed on the hard kitchen bench, throwing off the covers and putting on his hemp sandals at the sound of the early rooster's reveille.

Uncle Pascal had never smiled. He was the Latin type of father; the fearful master of the house, who, on returning from his labors, ate alone, served by his wife, who stood by with an expression of submission. But this grave, harsh mask of an omnipotent master concealed a boundless admiration for his son, who was his best work. How quickly he loaded a cart! How he perspired as he managed the hoe with a vigorous forward and backward motion that seemed to cleave him at the waist! Who could ride a pony like him, gracefully jumping on to his back by simply resting the toe of a sandal upon the hind legs of the animal?... He didn't touch wine, never got mixed up in a brawl, nor was he afraid of work. Through good luck he had pulled a high number in the military draft, and when the feast of San Juan came around he intended to marry a girl from a near-by farm,—a maiden that would bring with her a few pieces of earth when she came to the cabin of her new parents. Happiness; an honorable and peaceful continuation of the family traditions;

another *Caldera*, who, when Uncle Pascal grew old, would continue to work the lands that had been fructified by his ancestors, while a troop of little *Calderitas*, increasing in number each year, would play around the nag harnessed to the plow, eyeing with a certain awe their grandpa, his eyes watery from age and his words very concise, as he sat in the sun at the cabin door.

Christ! And how man's illusions vanish!... One Saturday, as Pascualet was coming home from his sweetheart's house, along one of the paths of the *huerta*, about midnight, a dog had bitten him; a wretched, silent animal that jumped out from behind a sluice; as the young man crouched to throw a stone at it, the dog bit into his shoulder. His mother, who used to wait for him on the nights when he went courting, burst into wailing when she saw the livid semicircle, with its red stain left by the dog's teeth, and she bustled about the hut preparing poultices and drinks.

The youth laughed at his mother's fears. "Quiet, mother, quiet!" It wasn't the first time that a dog had bitten him. His body still showed faint signs of bites that he had received in childhood, when he used to go through the *huerta* throwing stones at the dogs. Old *Caldera* spoke to him from bed, without displaying any emotion. On the following day he was to go to the veterinary and have his flesh cauterized by a burning iron. So he ordered, and there was nothing further to be said about the matter. The young man submitted without flinching to the operation, like a good, brave chap of the Valencian *huerta*. He had four days' rest in all, and even at that, his fondness for work caused him new sufferings and he aided his father with pain-tortured arm. Saturdays, when he came to his sweet-heart's farmhouse, she always asked after his health. "How's the bite getting along?" He would shrug his shoulders gleefully before the eyes of the maiden and the two would finally sit down in a corner of the kitchen, remaining in mute contemplation of each other, or speaking of the clothes and the bed for their future home, without daring to come close to each other; there they sat erect and solemn, leaving between their bodies a space "wide enough for a sickle to pass through," as the girl's father smilingly put it.

More than a month passed by. *Caldera's* wife was the only one that did not forget the accident. She followed her son about with anxious glances. Ah, sovereign queen! The *huerta* seemed to have been abandoned by God and His holy mother. Over at Templat's cabin a child was suffering the agonies of hell through having been bitten by a mad dog. All the *huerta* folk were running in terror to have a look at the poor crea-ture; a spectacle that she herself did not dare to gaze upon because she was thinking of her own son. If her Pascualet, as tall and sturdy as a tower, were to meet with the same fate as that unfortunate child!...

One day, at dawn, *Caldera's* son was unable to arise from his kitchen bench, and his mother helped him walk to the large nuptial bed, which occupied a part of the *estudi*, the best room in the cabin. He was feverish, and complained of acute pain in the spot where he had been bitten; an awful chill ran through his whole body, making his teeth chatter and veiling his eyes with a yellowish opacity. Don Jose, the oldest doctor in the *huerta*, came on his ancient mare, with his eternal recipe of purgatives for every class of illness, and bandages soaked in salt water for wounds. Upon examining the sick man he made a wry face. Bad! Bad! This was a more serious matter; they would have to go to the solemn doctors in Valencia, who knew more than he. *Caldera's* wife saw her husband harness the cart and compel Pascualet to get into it. The boy, relieved of his pain, smiled assent, saying that now he felt nothing more than a slight twinge. When they returned to the cabin the father seemed to be more at ease. A doctor from the city had pricked Pascualet's sore. He was a very serious gentleman, who gave Pascualet courage with his kind words, looking intently at him all the while, and expressing regret that he had waited so long before coming to him. For a week the two men made a daily trip to Valencia, but one morning the boy was unable to move. That crisis which made the poor mother groan with fear had returned with greater intensity than before. The boy's teeth knocked together, and he uttered a wail that stained the corners of his mouth with froth; his eyes seemed to swell, becoming yellow and protruding like huge grape seeds; he tried to pull himself together, writhing from the internal torture, and his mother hung upon his neck, shrieking with terror; meanwhile *Caldera*, grimly silent, seized his son's arms with tranquil strength, struggling to prevent his violent convulsions.

"My son! My son!" cried the mother. Ah, her son! Scarcely could she recognize him as she saw him in this condition. He seemed like another, as if only his former exterior had remained,—as if an infernal monster had lodged within and was martyrizing this flesh that had come out of her own womb, appearing at his eyes with livid flashes.

Afterwards came calm stupor, and all the women of the district gathered in the kitchen and deliberated upon the lot of the sick youth, cursing the city doctor and his diabolical incisions. It was his fault that the boy now lay thus; before the boy had submitted to the cure he had felt much better. The bandit! And the government never punished these wicked souls!... There were no other remedies than the old, true and tried ones,— the product of the experience of people who had lived years ago and thus knew much more. One of the neighbors went off to hunt up a certain witch, a miraculous doctor for dog-bites, serpent bites and scorpion-stings. Another brought a blind old goatherd, who could cure by the virtue of his mouth, simply by making some crosses of saliva over the ailing flesh. The drinks made of mountain herbs and the moist signs of the goatherd were looked upon as tokens of immediate cure, especially when they beheld the sick youth lie silent and motionless for several hours, looking at the ground with a certain amazement, as if he could feel within him the progress of something strange that grew and grew, gradually overpowering him. Then, when the crisis re-occurred, the doubt of the women began to rise, and new remedies were discussed. The youth's sweetheart came, with her large black eyes moistened by tears, and she advanced timidly until she came near to the sick boy. For the first time she dared to take his hand, blushing beneath her cinnamon-colored complexion at this audacious act. "How do you feel?" ... And he, so loving in other days, recoiled from her tender touch, turning his eyes away so that he should not see her, as if ashamed of his plight. His mother wept. Queen of heaven! He was very low; he was going to die. If only they could find out what dog it was that had bitten him, and cut out its tongue, using it for a miraculous plaster, as experienced persons advised!...

Throughout the *huerta* it seemed that God's own wrath had burst forth. Some dogs had bitten others; now nobody knew which were the dangerous ones and which the safe. All mad! The children were secluded in the cabins, spying with terrified glances upon the vast fields, through the half-open doors; mothers journeyed over the winding paths in close groups, uneasy, trembling, hastening their step whenever a bark sounded from behind the sluices of the canals; men eyed the domestic dogs with fear, intently watching their slavering mouths as they gasped or their sad eyes; the agile greyhound, their hunting companion,—the barking cur, guardian of the home,—the ugly mastiff who walked along tied to the cart, which he watched over during the master's absence,—all were placed under their owners' observation or coldly sacrificed behind the walls of the corral, without any display of emotion whatever.

"Here they come! Here they come!" was the shout passed along from cabin to cabin, announcing the patter of a pack of dogs, howling, ravenous, their bodies covered with mud, running about without finding rest, driven on day and night, with the madness of persecution in their eyes. The *huerta* seemed to shudder, closing the doors of all the houses and suddenly bristling with guns. Shots rang out from the sluices, from the high corn-fields, from cabin windows, and when the wanderers, repelled and persecuted on every side, in their mad gallop dashed toward the sea, as if they were attracted by the moist, invigorating air that was washed by the waves, the revenue-guards camped on the wide strip of beach brought their mausers to their cheeks and received them with a volley. The dogs retreated, escaping among the men who were approaching them musket in hand, and one or another of them would be stretched out at the edge of the canal. At night, the noisy gloom of the plain was broken by the sight of distant flashes and the sound of discharges. Every shape that moved in the darkness was the target for a bullet; the muffled howls that sounded in the vicinity of the cabins were answered by shots. The men were afraid of this common terror, and avoided meeting.

No sooner did night fall than the *huerta* was left without a light, without a person upon the roads, as if death had taken possession of the dismal plain, so green and smiling under the sun. A single red spot, a tear of light, trembled in this obscurity. It was *Caldera's* cabin, where the women, squatting upon the floor, around the kitchen lamp, sighed with fright, anticipating the strident shriek of the sick youth,—the chattering of his teeth, the violent contortions of his body whenever he was seized with convulsions, struggling to repel the arms that tried to quiet him.

The mother hung upon the neck of that raving patient who struck terror to men. She scarcely knew him; he was somebody else, with those eyes that popped out of their sockets, his livid or blackish countenance, his writhings, like that of a tortured animal, showing his tongue as he gasped through bubbles of froth in the agonies of an insatiable thirst. He begged for death in heart-rending shrieks; he struck his head against the wall; he tried to bite; but even so, he was her child and she did not feel the fear experienced by the others. His menacing mouth withdrew before the wan face that was moistened with tears. "Mother! Mother!" He recognized her in his lucid moments. She need not fear him; he would never bite her. And as if he must sink his teeth into something or other to glut his rage, he bit into his arms until the blood came.

"My son! My son!" moaned the mother and she wiped the deadly froth from his lips, afterwards carrying the handkerchief to her eyes, without fear of contagion. *Caldera*, in his solemn gravity, paid no heed to the sufferer's threatening eyes, which were fixed upon him with an impulse of attack. The boy had lost his awe of his father.

That powerful man, however, facing the peril of his son's mouth, thrust him back into bed whenever the madman tried to flee, as if he must spread everywhere the horrible affliction that was devouring his entrails.

No longer were the crises followed by extended intervals of calm. They became almost continuous, and the victim writhed about, clawed and bleeding from his own bites, his face almost black, his eyes tremulous and yellow, looking like some monstrous beast set apart from all the human species. The old doctor had stopped asking about the youth. What was the use? It was all over. The women wept hopelessly. Death was certain. They only bewailed the long hours, perhaps days, of horrible torture that poor Pascualet would have to undergo.

Caldera was unable to find among his relatives or friends any men brave enough to help him restrain the sufferer in his violent moments. They all looked with terror at the door to the *estudi*, as if behind it were concealed the greatest of dangers. To go shooting through roads and canals was man's work. A stab could be returned; one bullet could answer another; but ah! that frothing mouth which killed with a bite!... that incurable disease which made men writhe in endless agony, like a lizard sliced by a hoe!

He no longer knew his mother. In his final moments of lucidity he had thrust her away with loving brusqueness. She must go!... Let him not see her again!... He feared to do her harm! The poor woman's friends dragged her out of the room, forcing her to remain motionless, like her son, in a corner of the kitchen. *Caldera*, with a supreme effort of his dying will, tied the agonizing youth to the bed. His beetling brows trembled and the tears made him blink as he tied the coarse knots of the rope, fastening the youth to the bed upon which he had been born. He felt as if he were preparing his son for burial and had begun to dig his grave. The victim twisted in wild contortions under the father's strong arms; the parent had to make a powerful effort to subdue him under the rope that sank into his flesh.... To have lived so many years only to behold himself at last obliged to perform such a task! To give life to a creature, only to pray that it might be extinguished as soon as possible, horrified by so much useless pain!... Good God in heaven! Why not put an end to the poor boy at once, since his death was now inevitable?...

He closed the door of the sick room, fleeing from the rasping shriek that set everybody's hair on end; but the madman's panting continued to sound in the silence of the cabin, accompanied by the lamentations of the mother and the weeping of the other women grouped around the lamp that had just been lighted.

Caldera stamped upon the floor. Let the women be silent! But for the first time he beheld himself disobeyed, and he left the cabin, fleeing from this chorus of grief.

Night descended. His gaze wandered toward the thin yellow band that was visible on the horizon, marking the flight of day. Above his head shone the stars. From the other homes, which were scarcely visible, resounded the neighing of horses, barking, and the clucking of fowl—the last signs of animal life before it sank to rest. That primitive man felt an impression of emptiness amid the Nature which was insensible and blind to the sufferings of its creatures. Of what concern to the points of light that looked down upon him from above could be that which he was now going through?... All creatures were equal; the beasts that disturbed the silence of dusk before falling asleep, and that poor youth similar to him, who now lay fettered, writhing in the worst of agony. How many illusions his life had contained!... And with a mere bite, a wretched animal kicked about by all men could finish them all. And no remedy existed in heaven or upon earth!...

Once again the distant shriek of the sufferer came to his ears from the open window of the *estudi*. The tenderness of his early days of paternity emerged from the depths of his soul. He recalled the nights he had spent awake in that room, walking up and down, holding in his arms the little child that was crying from the pains of infancy's illness. Now he lay crying, too, but without hope, in the agonies of a hell that had come before its time, and at last ... death.

His countenance grew frightened, and he raised his hands to his forehead as if trying to drive away a troublesome thought. Then he appeared to deliberate ... Why not?...

"To end his suffering ... to end his suffering!"

He went back to the cabin, only to come out at once with his old double-barrelled musket, and he hastened to the little window of the sick room as if he feared to lose his determination; he thrust the gun through the opening.

Again he heard the agonizing panting, the chattering of teeth, the horrible shriek, now very near, as if he were at the victim's bedside. His eyes, accustomed to the darkness, saw the bed at the back of the gloomy room, and the form that lay writhing in it—the pale spot of the face, appearing and disappearing as the sick man twisted about desperately.

The father was frightened at the trembling of his hands and the agitation of his pulse; he, the son of the *huerta*, without any other diversion than the hunt, accustomed to shoot down birds almost without aiming at them.

The wailing of the poor mother brought back to his memory other groans of long long ago—twenty-two years before—when she was giving birth to her only son upon that same bed.

To come to such an end!... His eyes, gazing heavenward, saw a black sky, intensely black, with not a star in sight, and obscured by his tears....

"Lord! To end his sufferings! To end his sufferings!"

And repeating these words he pressed the musket against his shoulder, seeking the lock with a tremulous finger.... Bang! Bang!

www.ingramcontent.com/pod-product-compliance
Lightning Source LLC
Chambersburg PA
CBHW030542180626
46810CB00005B/1970